J

D1177542

STONE ARCH BOOKS
a capstone imprint

Stone Arch Books™

Published in 2014
A Capstone Imprint
1710 Roe Crest Drive
North Mankato, MN 56003
www.capstonepub.com

Originally published by DC Comics in the U.S. in
single magazine form as The Batman Strikes! #3.
Copyright © 2014 DC Comics. All Rights Reserved.

DC Comics
1700 Broadway, New York, NY 10019
A Warner Bros. Entertainment Company
Printed in China by Nordica.
1013/CAZ1301918
092013   007744NORD514

Cataloging-in-Publication Data is available at the
Library of Congress website:
ISBN: 978-1-4342-6485-5 (library binding)

Summary: In this adventure starring the Joker,
criminals are getting caught, then disappearing--but
where? When the Joker plays police officer, it's
"Outlaw and Disorder" for Gotham City and Batman!

STONE ARCH BOOKS
Ashley C. Andersen Zantop *Publisher*
Michael Dahl *Editorial Director*
Sean Tulien *Editor*
Heather Kindseth *Creative Director*
Bob Lentz *Designer*
Kathy McColley *Production Specialist*

DC COMICS
Joan Hilty & Harvey Richards *Original U.S. Editors*
Jeff Matsuda & Dave McCaig *Cover Artists*

JOKER'S WILD!

BILL MATHENY ....WRITER
CHRISTOPHER JONES ....PENCILLER
TERRY BEATTY...INKER
HEROIC AGE...COLORIST
PAT BROSSEAU ....LETTERER

BATMAN CREATED BY
BOB KANE

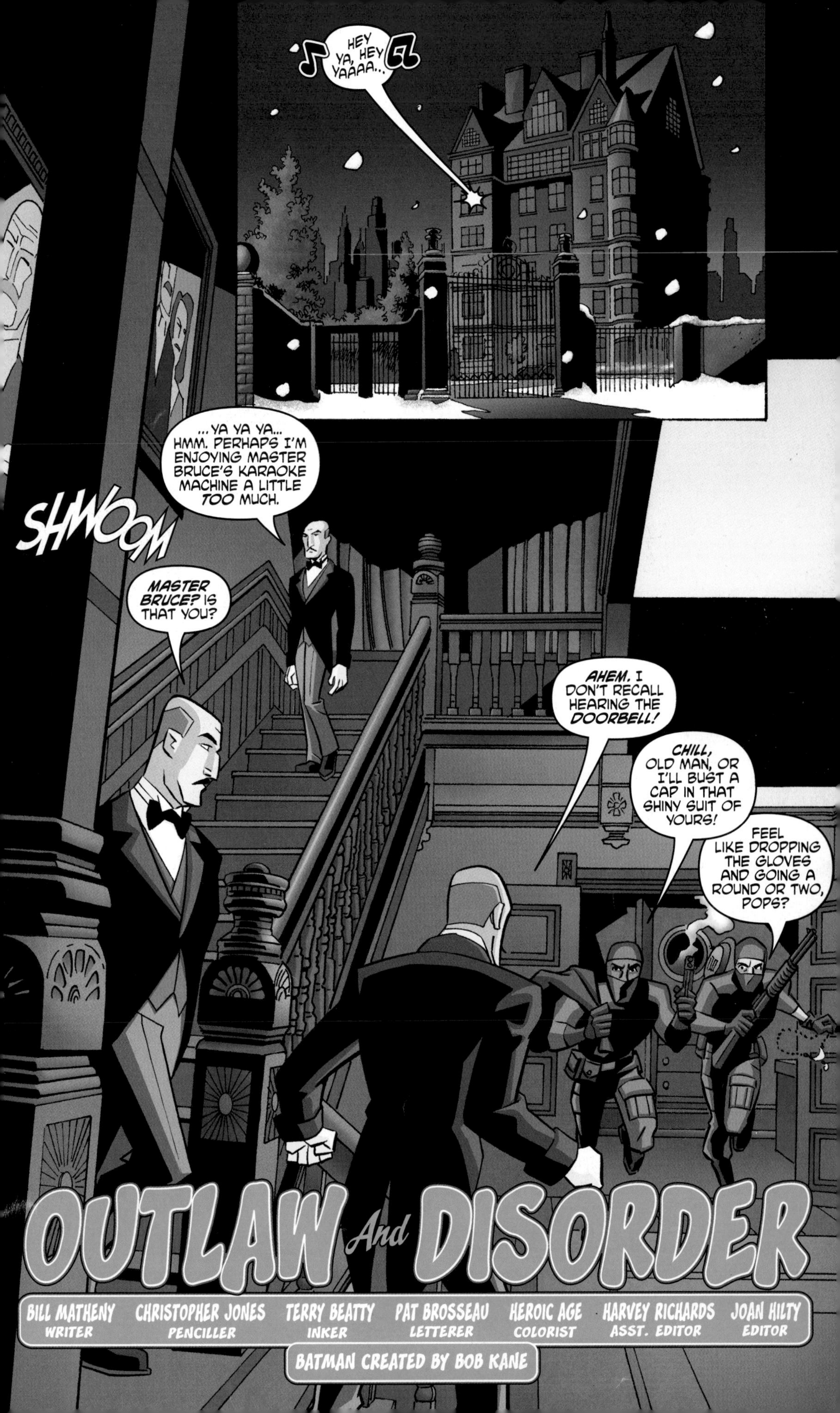
HEY YA, HEY YAAAA...
...YA YA YA... HMM. PERHAPS I'M ENJOYING MASTER BRUCE'S KARAOKE MACHINE A LITTLE TOO MUCH.
SHWOOM
MASTER BRUCE? IS THAT YOU?
AHEM. I DON'T RECALL HEARING THE DOORBELL!
CHILL, OLD MAN, OR I'LL BUST A CAP IN THAT SHINY SUIT OF YOURS!
FEEL LIKE DROPPING THE GLOVES AND GOING A ROUND OR TWO, POPS?
OUTLAW And DISORDER
BILL MATHENY WRITER
CHRISTOPHER JONES PENCILLER
TERRY BEATTY INKER
PAT BROSSEAU LETTERER
HEROIC AGE COLORIST
HARVEY RICHARDS ASST. EDITOR
JOAN HILTY EDITOR
BATMAN CREATED BY BOB KANE

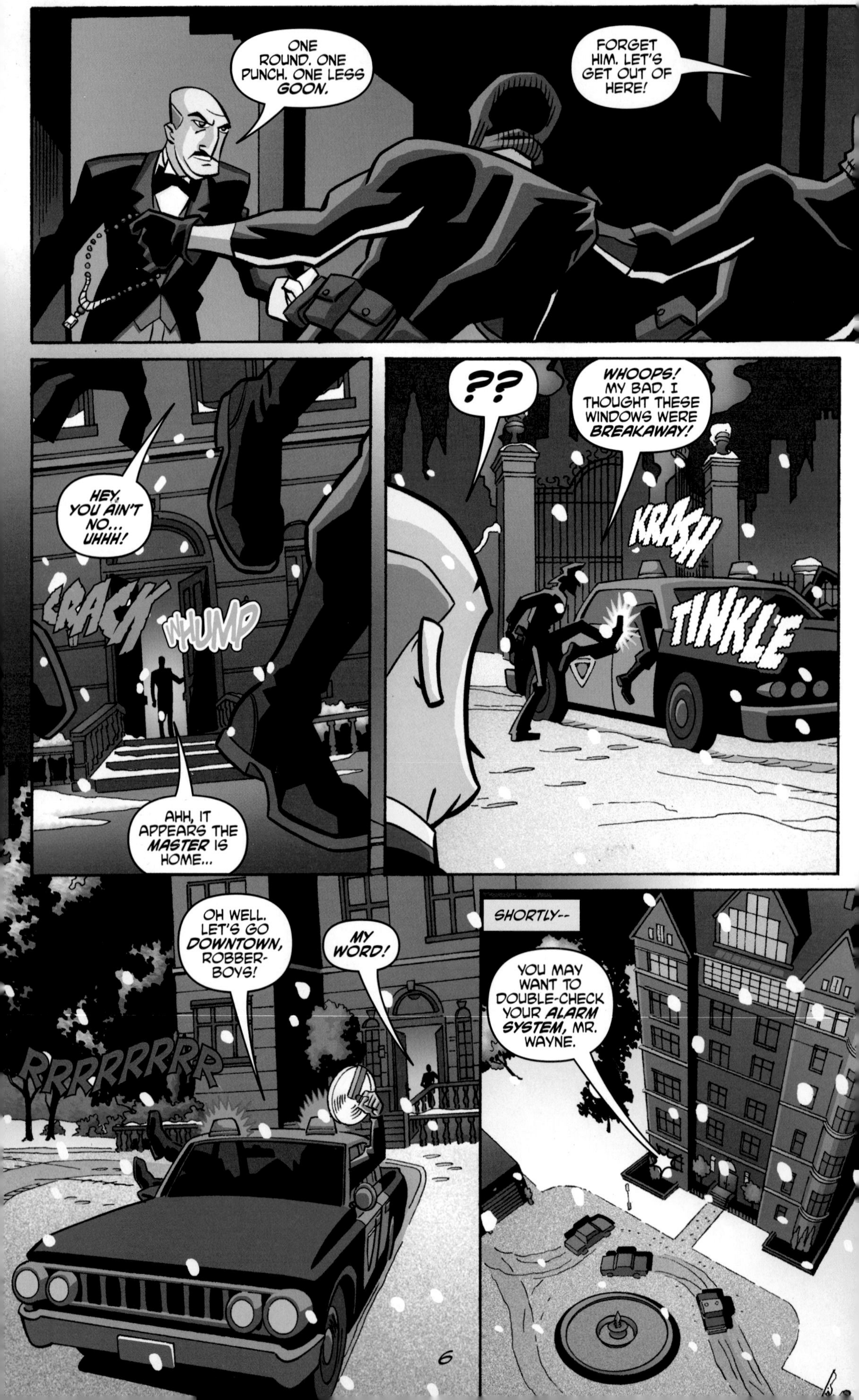
ONE ROUND. ONE PUNCH. ONE LESS GOON.
FORGET HIM. LET'S GET OUT OF HERE!
HEY, YOU AIN'T NO... UHHH!
CRACK
WHUMP
AHH, IT APPEARS THE MASTER IS HOME...
??
WHOOPS! MY BAD. I THOUGHT THESE WINDOWS WERE BREAKAWAY!
KRASH
TINKLE
OH WELL. LET'S GO DOWNTOWN, ROBBER-BOYS!
MY WORD!
RRRRRRRRR
SHORTLY--
YOU MAY WANT TO DOUBLE-CHECK YOUR ALARM SYSTEM, MR. WAYNE.

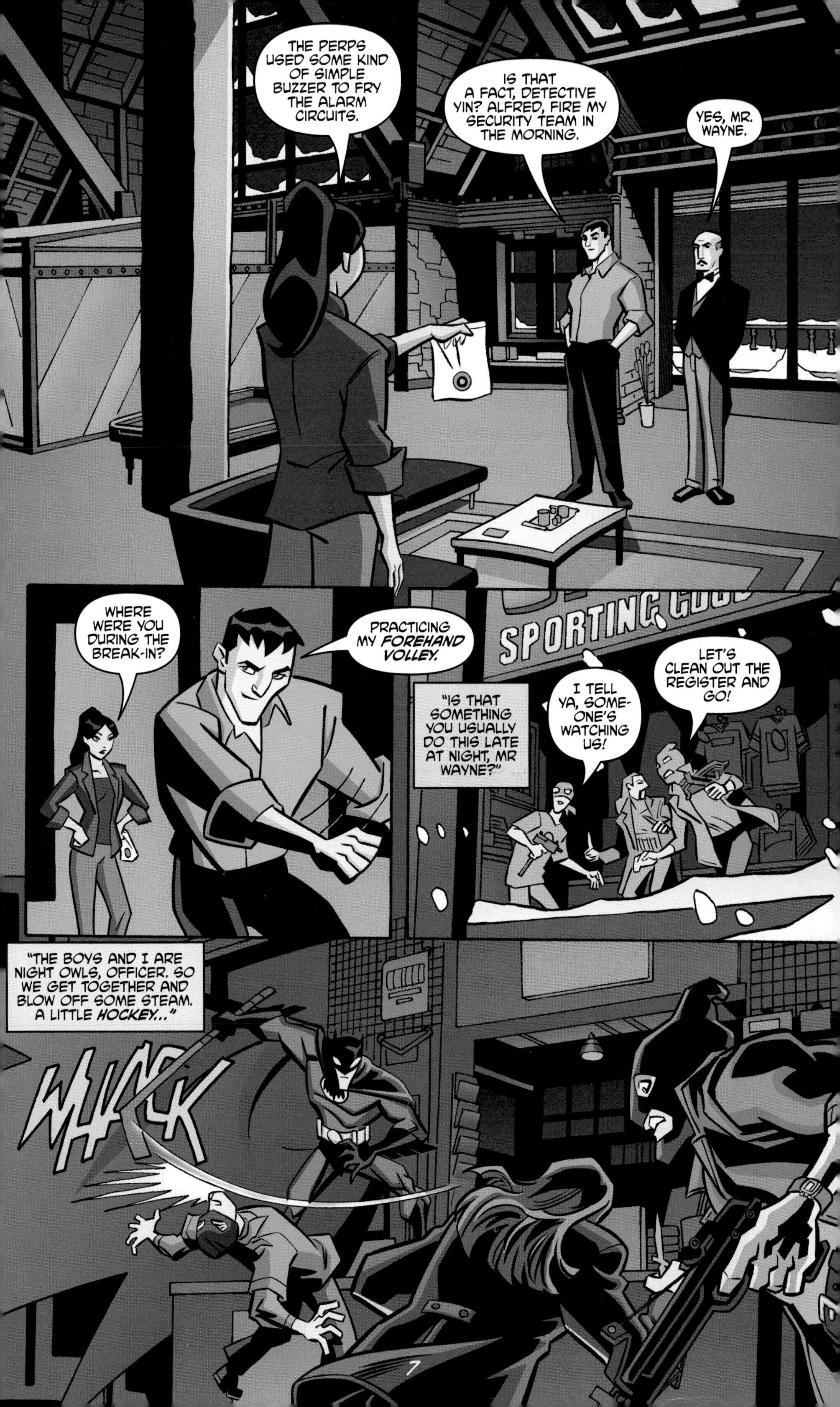

THE PERPS USED SOME KIND OF SIMPLE BUZZER TO FRY THE ALARM CIRCUITS.
IS THAT A FACT, DETECTIVE YIN? ALFRED, FIRE MY SECURITY TEAM IN THE MORNING.
YES, MR. WAYNE.
WHERE WERE YOU DURING THE BREAK-IN?
PRACTICING MY *FOREHAND VOLLEY.*
SPORTING GOO
"IS THAT SOMETHING YOU USUALLY DO THIS LATE AT NIGHT, MR WAYNE?"
I TELL YA, SOME-ONE'S WATCHING US!
LET'S CLEAN OUT THE REGISTER AND GO!
"THE BOYS AND I ARE NIGHT OWLS, OFFICER. SO WE GET TOGETHER AND BLOW OFF SOME STEAM. A LITTLE *HOCKEY...*"
WHACK

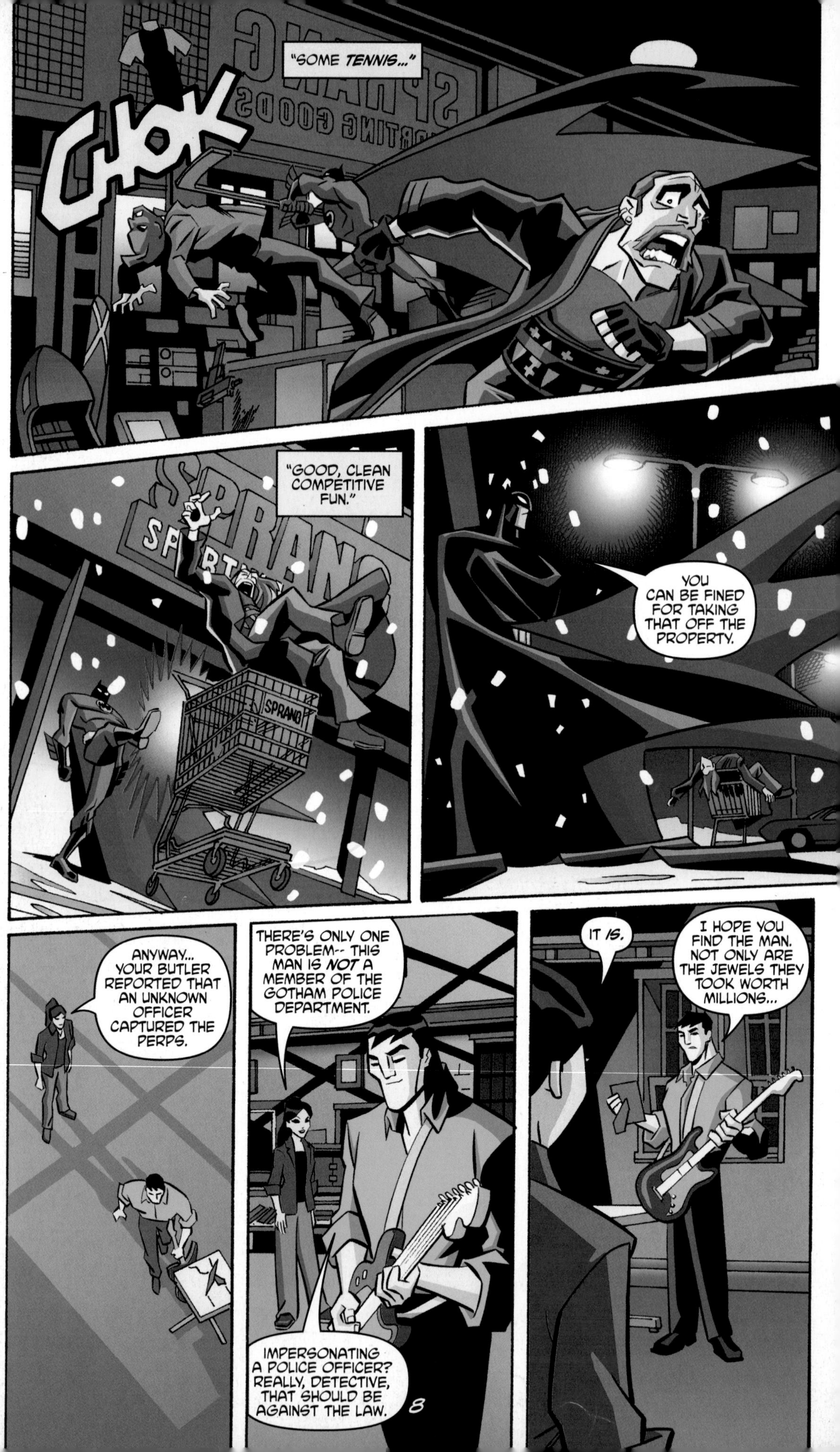
"SOME TENNIS..."
CHOK
"GOOD, CLEAN COMPETITIVE FUN."
SPRANG
YOU CAN BE FINED FOR TAKING THAT OFF THE PROPERTY.
ANYWAY... YOUR BUTLER REPORTED THAT AN UNKNOWN OFFICER CAPTURED THE PERPS.
THERE'S ONLY ONE PROBLEM-- THIS MAN IS NOT A MEMBER OF THE GOTHAM POLICE DEPARTMENT.
IMPERSONATING A POLICE OFFICER? REALLY, DETECTIVE, THAT SHOULD BE AGAINST THE LAW.
IT IS.
I HOPE YOU FIND THE MAN. NOT ONLY ARE THE JEWELS THEY TOOK WORTH MILLIONS...

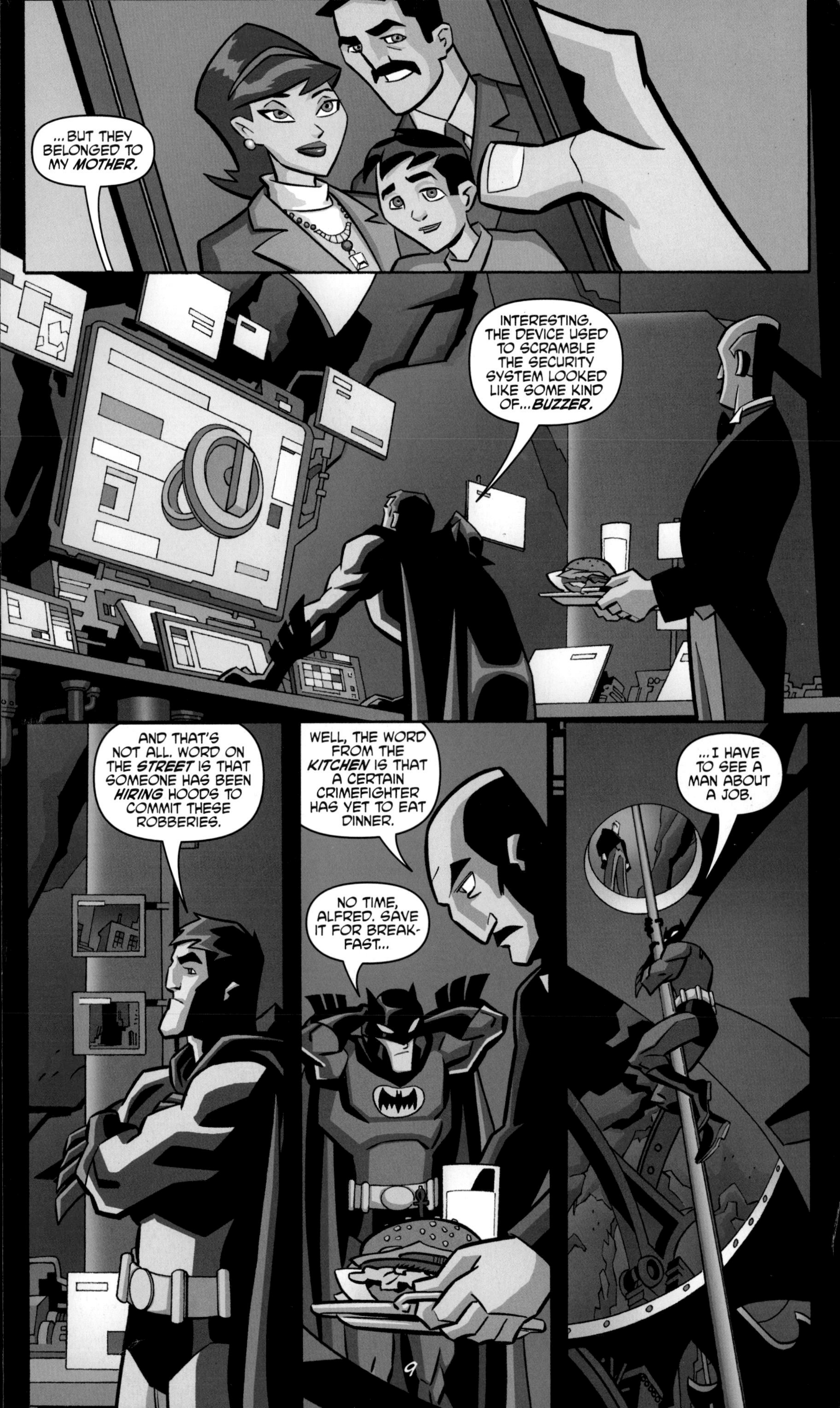

...BUT THEY BELONGED TO MY *MOTHER.*
INTERESTING. THE DEVICE USED TO SCRAMBLE THE SECURITY SYSTEM LOOKED LIKE SOME KIND OF...*BUZZER.*
AND THAT'S NOT ALL. WORD ON THE *STREET* IS THAT SOMEONE HAS BEEN *HIRING* HOODS TO COMMIT THESE ROBBERIES.
WELL, THE WORD FROM THE *KITCHEN* IS THAT A CERTAIN CRIMEFIGHTER HAS YET TO EAT DINNER.
NO TIME, ALFRED. SAVE IT FOR BREAK-FAST...
...I HAVE TO SEE A MAN ABOUT A JOB.

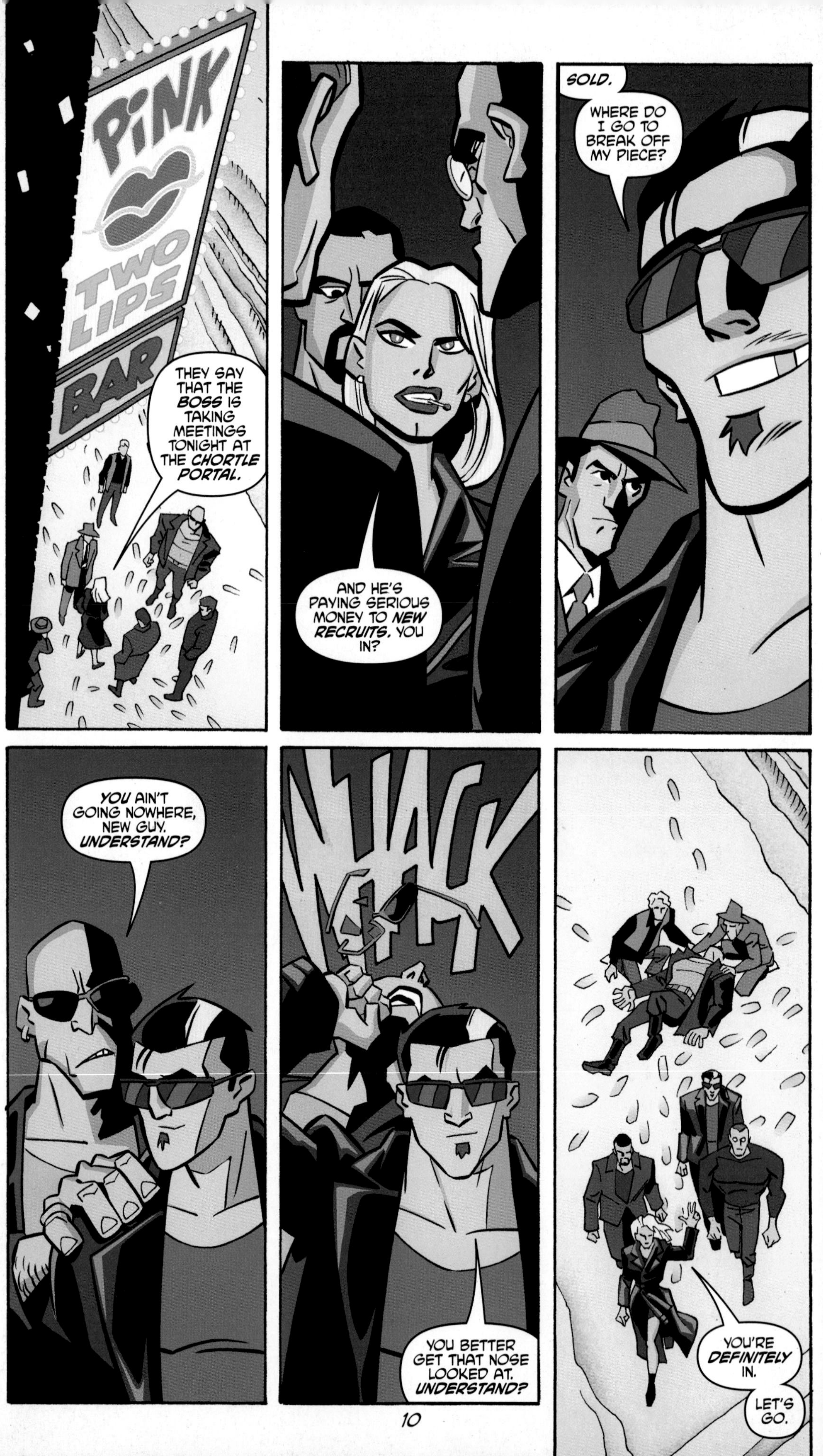
PINK
TWO LIPS
BAR
THEY SAY THAT THE BOSS IS TAKING MEETINGS TONIGHT AT THE CHORTLE PORTAL.
AND HE'S PAYING SERIOUS MONEY TO NEW RECRUITS. YOU IN?
SOLD.
WHERE DO I GO TO BREAK OFF MY PIECE?
YOU AIN'T GOING NOWHERE, NEW GUY. UNDERSTAND?
WHACK
YOU BETTER GET THAT NOSE LOOKED AT. UNDERSTAND?
YOU'RE DEFINITELY IN.
LET'S GO.

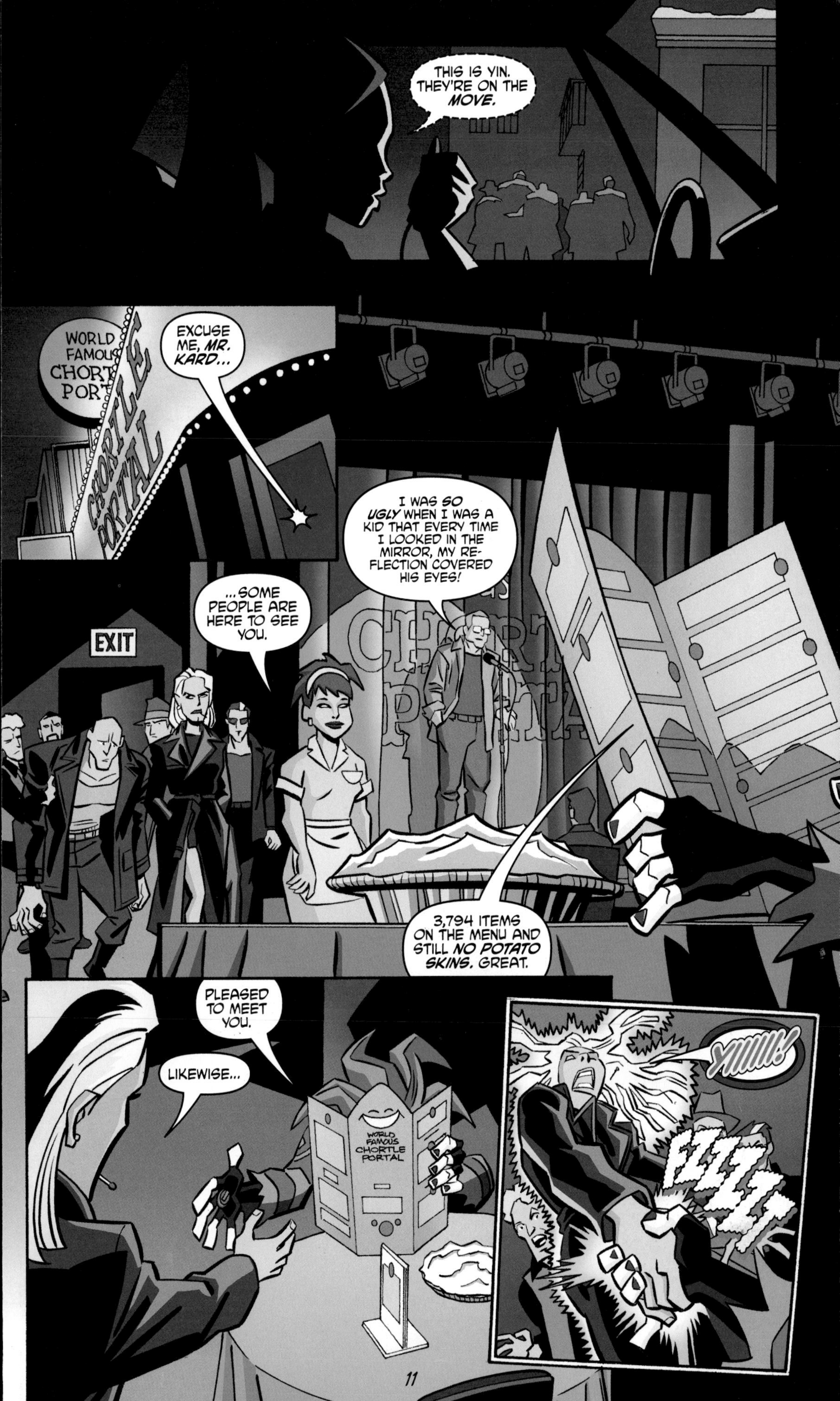
THIS IS YIN. THEY'RE ON THE *MOVE.*
WORLD FAMOUS CHORTLE PORTAL
CHORTLE PORTAL
EXCUSE ME, *MR. KARD*...
I WAS *SO UGLY* WHEN I WAS A KID THAT EVERY TIME I LOOKED IN THE MIRROR, MY RE-FLECTION COVERED HIS EYES!
EXIT
...SOME PEOPLE ARE HERE TO SEE YOU.
3,794 ITEMS ON THE MENU AND STILL *NO POTATO SKINS.* GREAT.
PLEASED TO MEET YOU.
LIKEWISE...
WORLD FAMOUS CHORTLE PORTAL
YIIIII!
ZZZZT

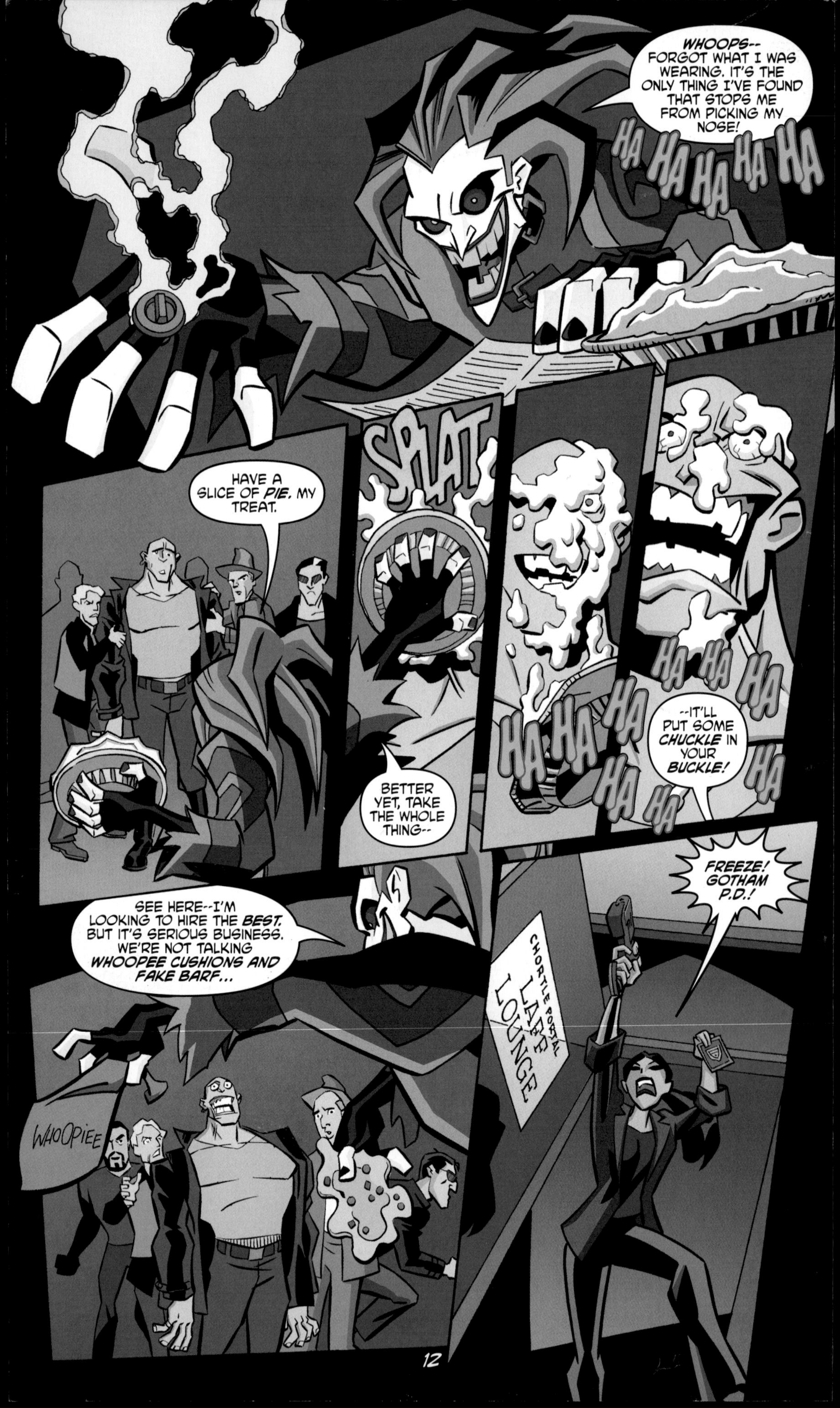

WHOOPS-- FORGOT WHAT I WAS WEARING. IT'S THE ONLY THING I'VE FOUND THAT STOPS ME FROM PICKING MY NOSE!
HA HA HA HA HA
HAVE A SLICE OF PIE. MY TREAT.
SPLAT
BETTER YET, TAKE THE WHOLE THING--
HA HA HA HA HA HA HA HA HA
--IT'LL PUT SOME CHUCKLE IN YOUR BUCKLE!
SEE HERE--I'M LOOKING TO HIRE THE BEST. BUT IT'S SERIOUS BUSINESS. WE'RE NOT TALKING WHOOPEE CUSHIONS AND FAKE BARF...
WHOOPIEE
CHORTLE PORTAL LAFF LOUNGE
FREEZE! GOTHAM P.D.!

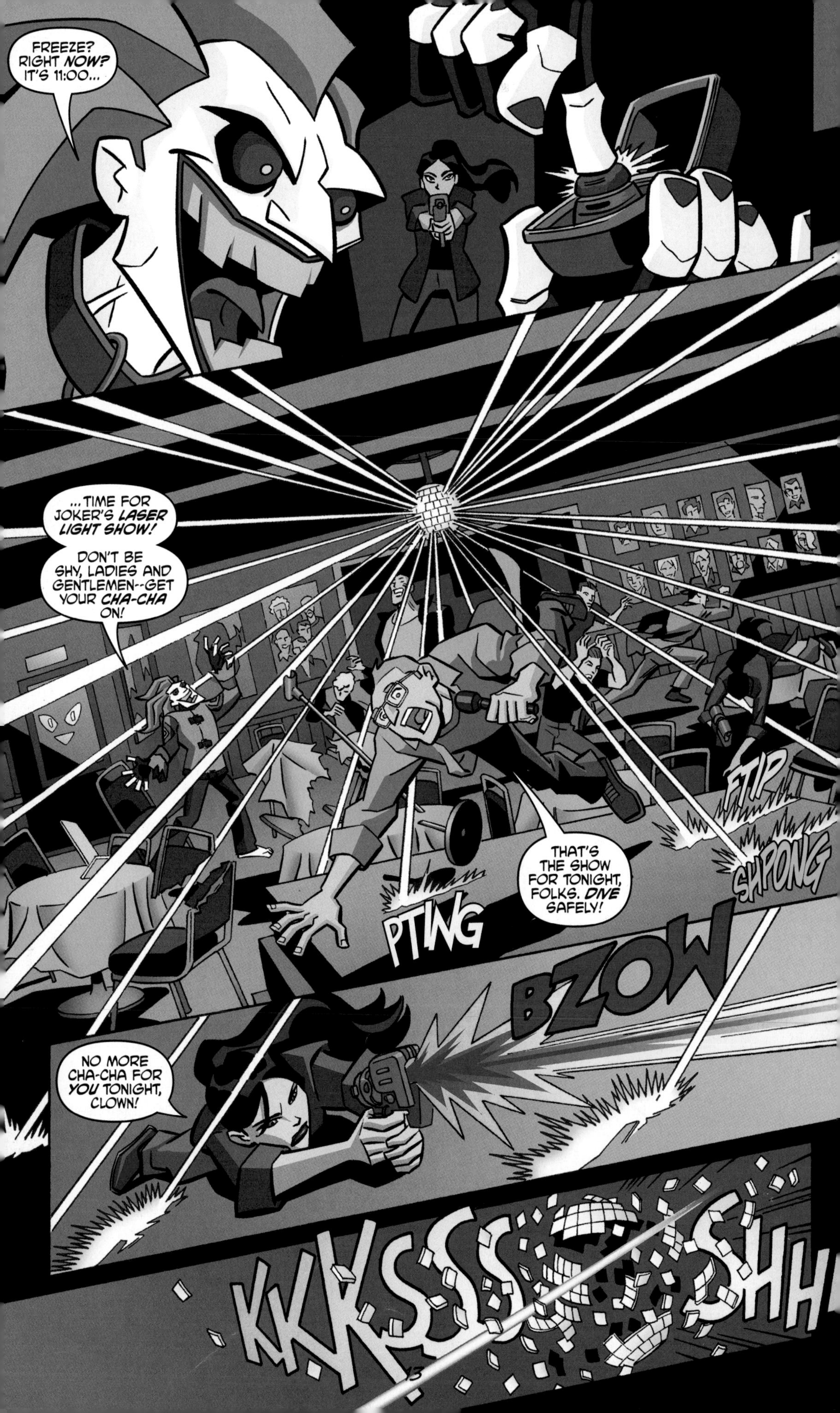

FREEZE? RIGHT NOW? IT'S 11:00...
...TIME FOR JOKER'S LASER LIGHT SHOW!
DON'T BE SHY, LADIES AND GENTLEMEN--GET YOUR CHA-CHA ON!
FTIP
SHPONG
THAT'S THE SHOW FOR TONIGHT, FOLKS. DIVE SAFELY!
PTING
BZOW
NO MORE CHA-CHA FOR YOU TONIGHT, CLOWN!
KKKSSSSSHH

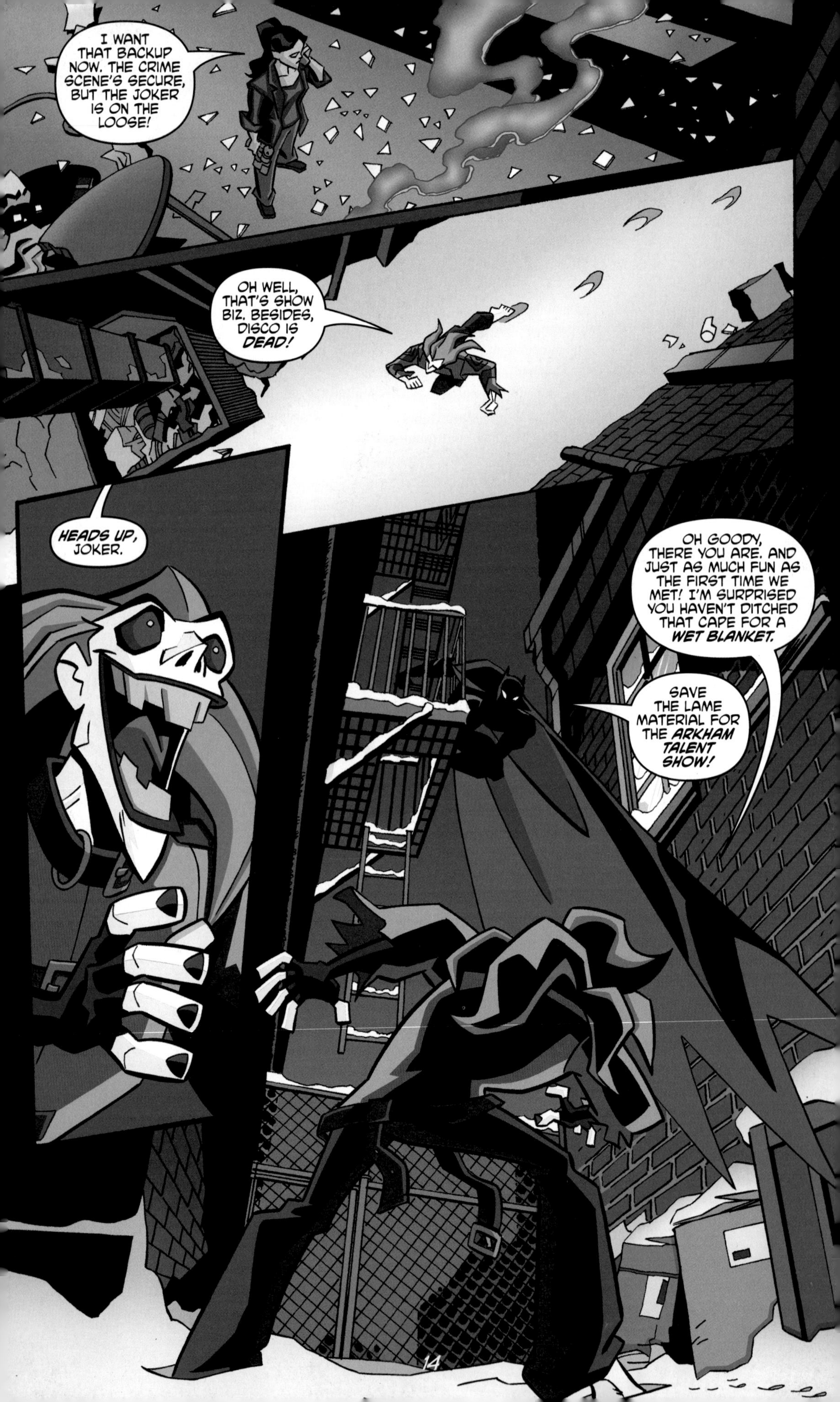

I WANT THAT BACKUP NOW. THE CRIME SCENE'S SECURE, BUT THE JOKER IS ON THE LOOSE!
OH WELL, THAT'S SHOW BIZ. BESIDES, DISCO IS *DEAD!*
HEADS UP, JOKER.
OH GOODY, THERE YOU ARE. AND JUST AS MUCH FUN AS THE FIRST TIME WE MET! I'M SURPRISED YOU HAVEN'T DITCHED THAT CAPE FOR A *WET BLANKET.*
SAVE THE LAME MATERIAL FOR THE *ARKHAM TALENT SHOW!*

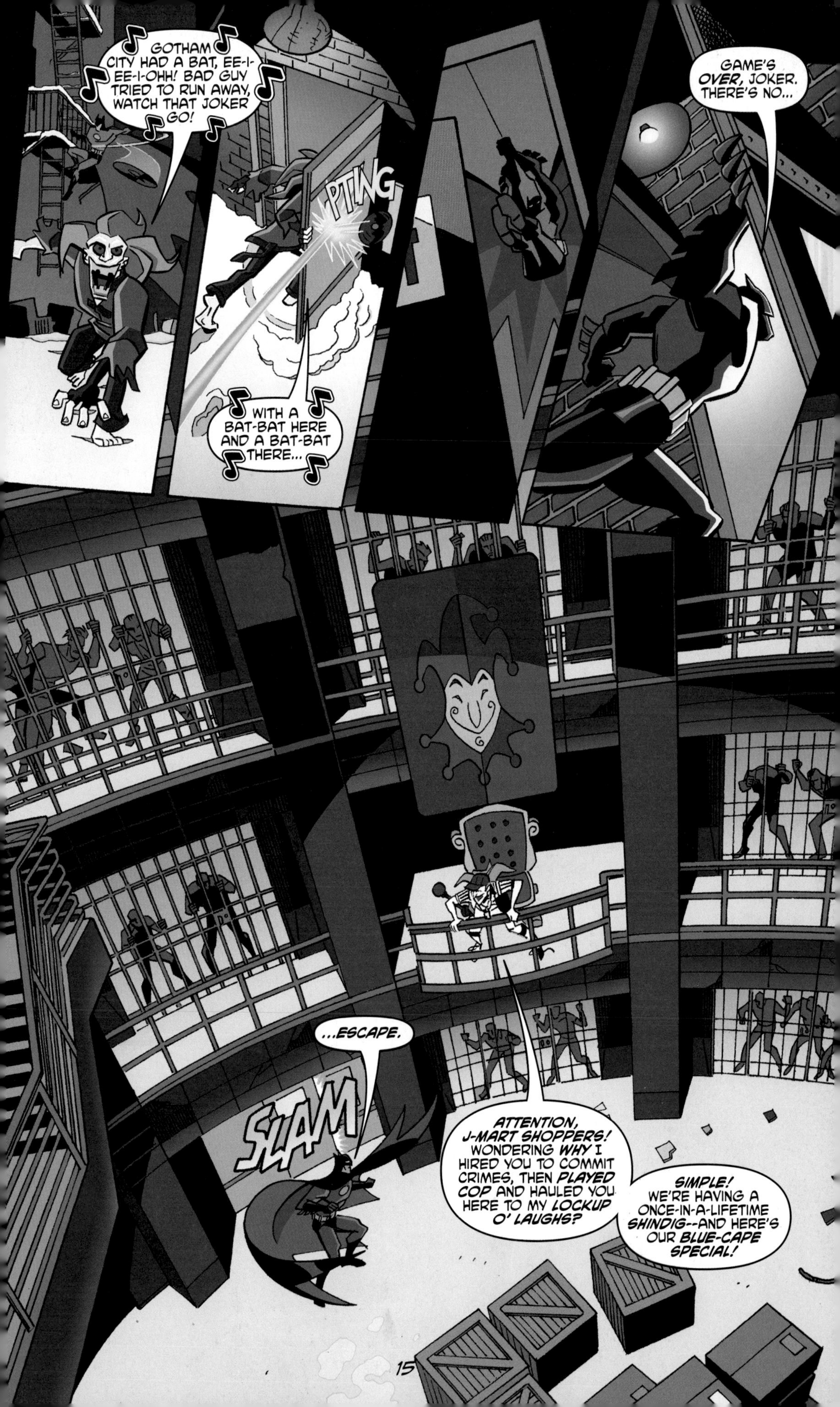
GOTHAM CITY HAD A BAT, EE-I-EE-I-OHH! BAD GUY TRIED TO RUN AWAY, WATCH THAT JOKER GO!
PTING
WITH A BAT-BAT HERE AND A BAT-BAT THERE...
GAME'S OVER, JOKER. THERE'S NO...
...ESCAPE.
SLAM
ATTENTION, J-MART SHOPPERS! WONDERING WHY I HIRED YOU TO COMMIT CRIMES, THEN PLAYED COP AND HAULED YOU HERE TO MY LOCKUP O' LAUGHS?
SIMPLE! WE'RE HAVING A ONCE-IN-A-LIFETIME SHINDIG--AND HERE'S OUR BLUE-CAPE SPECIAL!

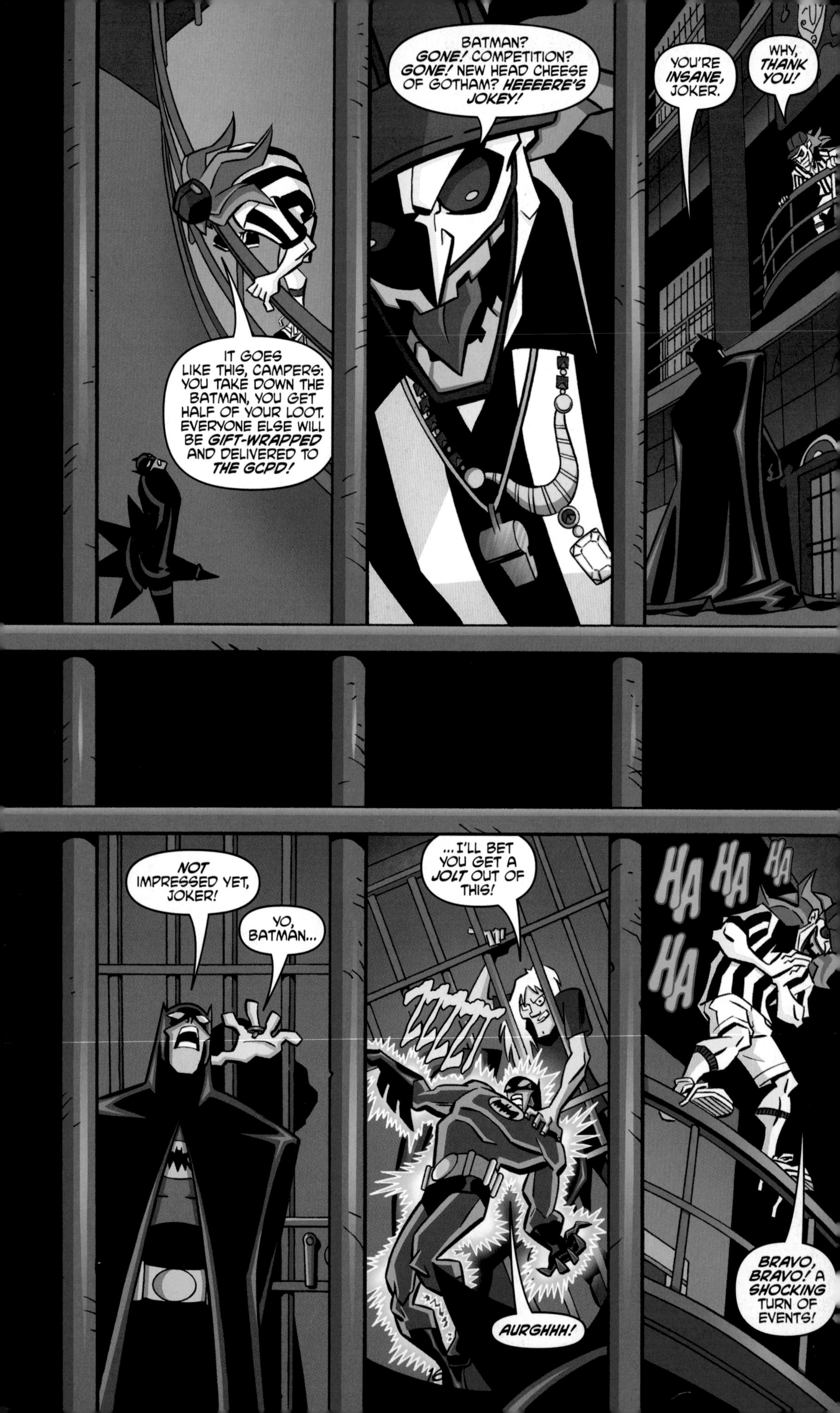
IT GOES LIKE THIS, CAMPERS: YOU TAKE DOWN THE BATMAN, YOU GET HALF OF YOUR LOOT. EVERYONE ELSE WILL BE GIFT-WRAPPED AND DELIVERED TO THE GCPD!
BATMAN? GONE! COMPETITION? GONE! NEW HEAD CHEESE OF GOTHAM? HEEEERE'S JOKEY!
YOU'RE INSANE, JOKER.
WHY, THANK YOU!
NOT IMPRESSED YET, JOKER!
YO, BATMAN...
...I'LL BET YOU GET A JOLT OUT OF THIS!
ZZZZT
AURGHHH!
HA HA HA
HA
BRAVO, BRAVO! A SHOCKING TURN OF EVENTS!

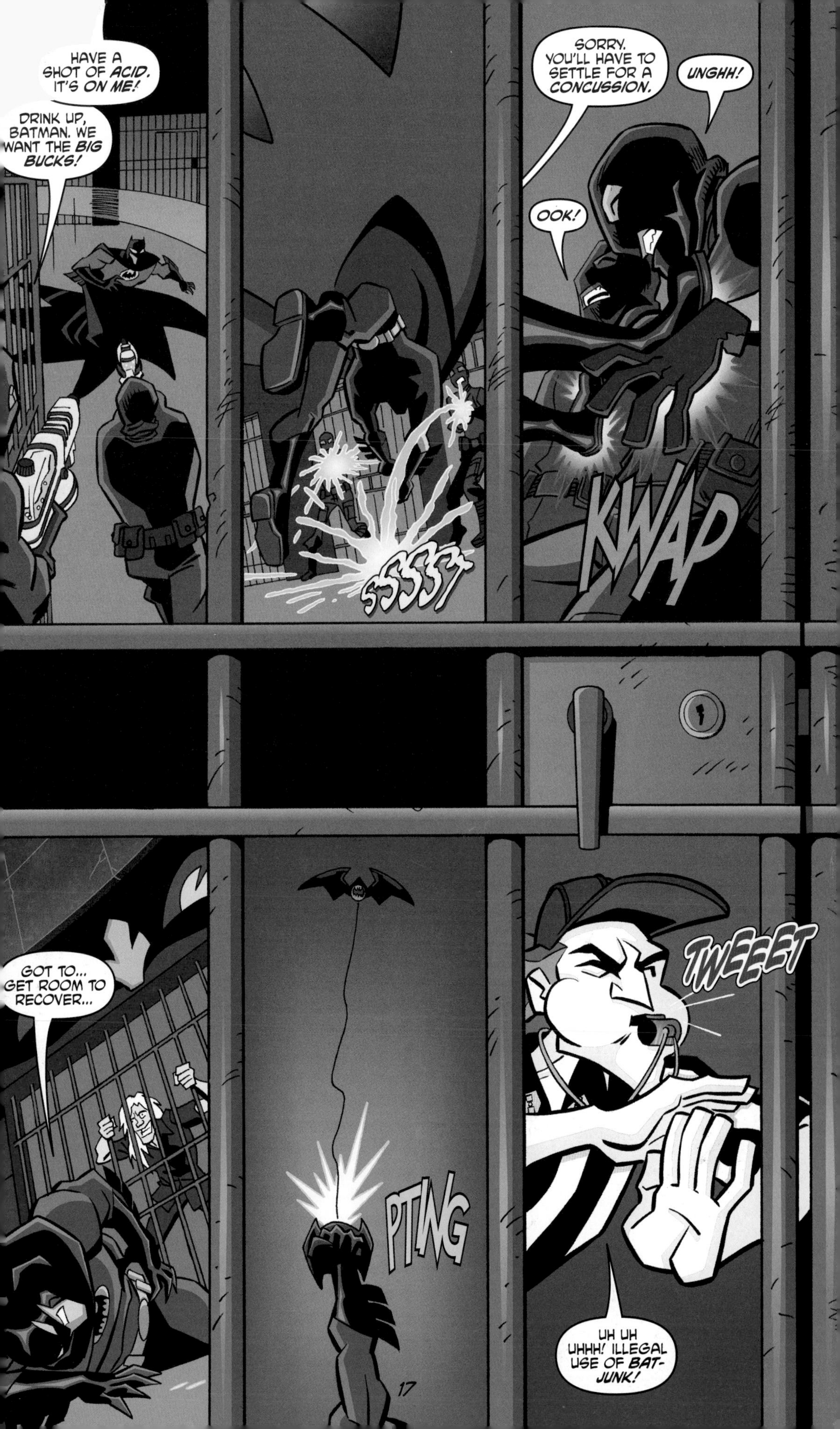
HAVE A SHOT OF *ACID*. IT'S *ON ME!*
DRINK UP, BATMAN. WE WANT THE *BIG BUCKS!*
SSSSST
SORRY. YOU'LL HAVE TO SETTLE FOR A *CONCUSSION*.
UNGHH!
OOK!
KWAP
GOT TO... GET ROOM TO RECOVER...
PTING
TWEEEET
UH UH UHHH! ILLEGAL USE OF *BAT-JUNK!*
17

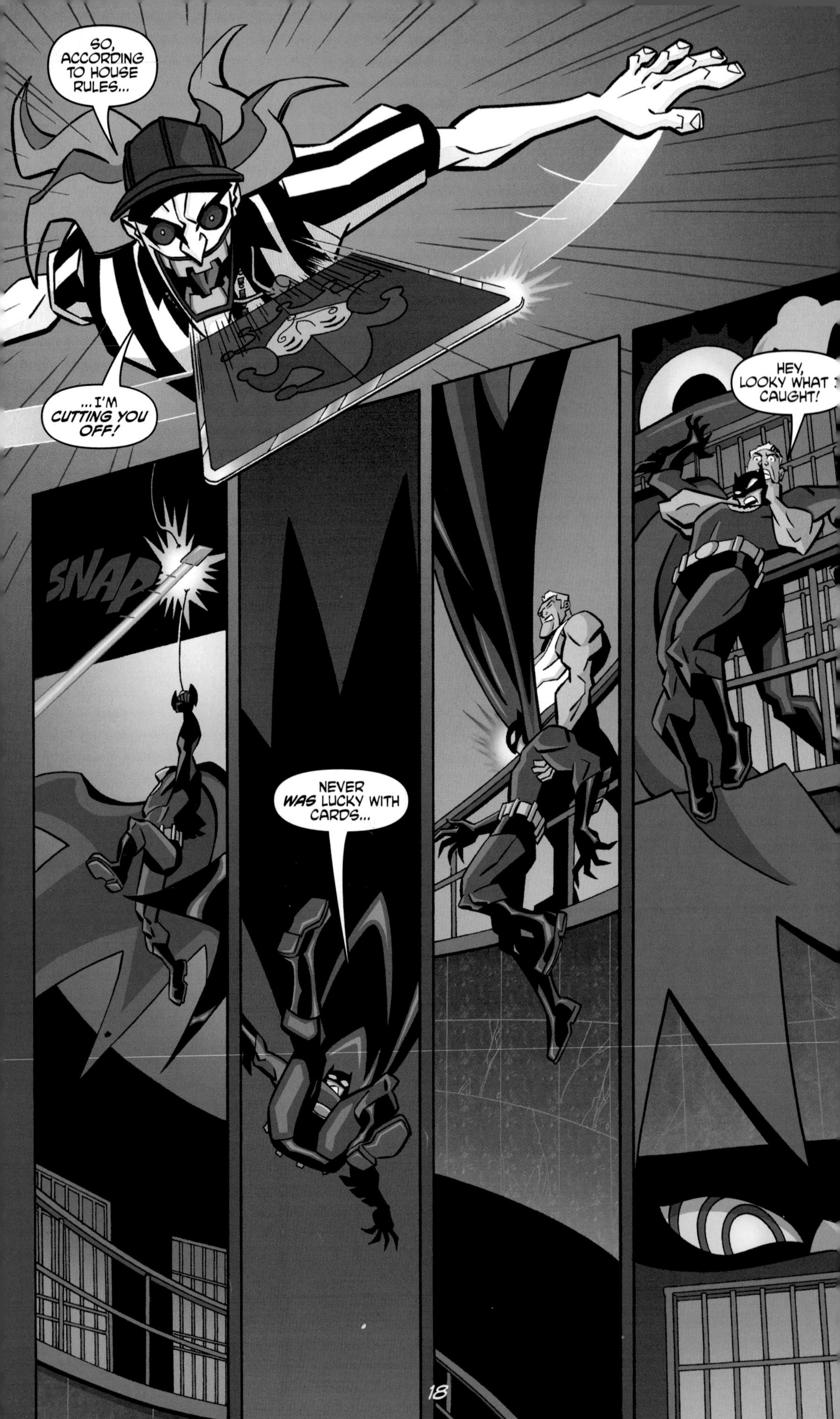
SO, ACCORDING TO HOUSE RULES...
...I'M *CUTTING YOU OFF!*
SNAP
NEVER *WAS* LUCKY WITH CARDS...
HEY, LOOKY WHAT I CAUGHT!

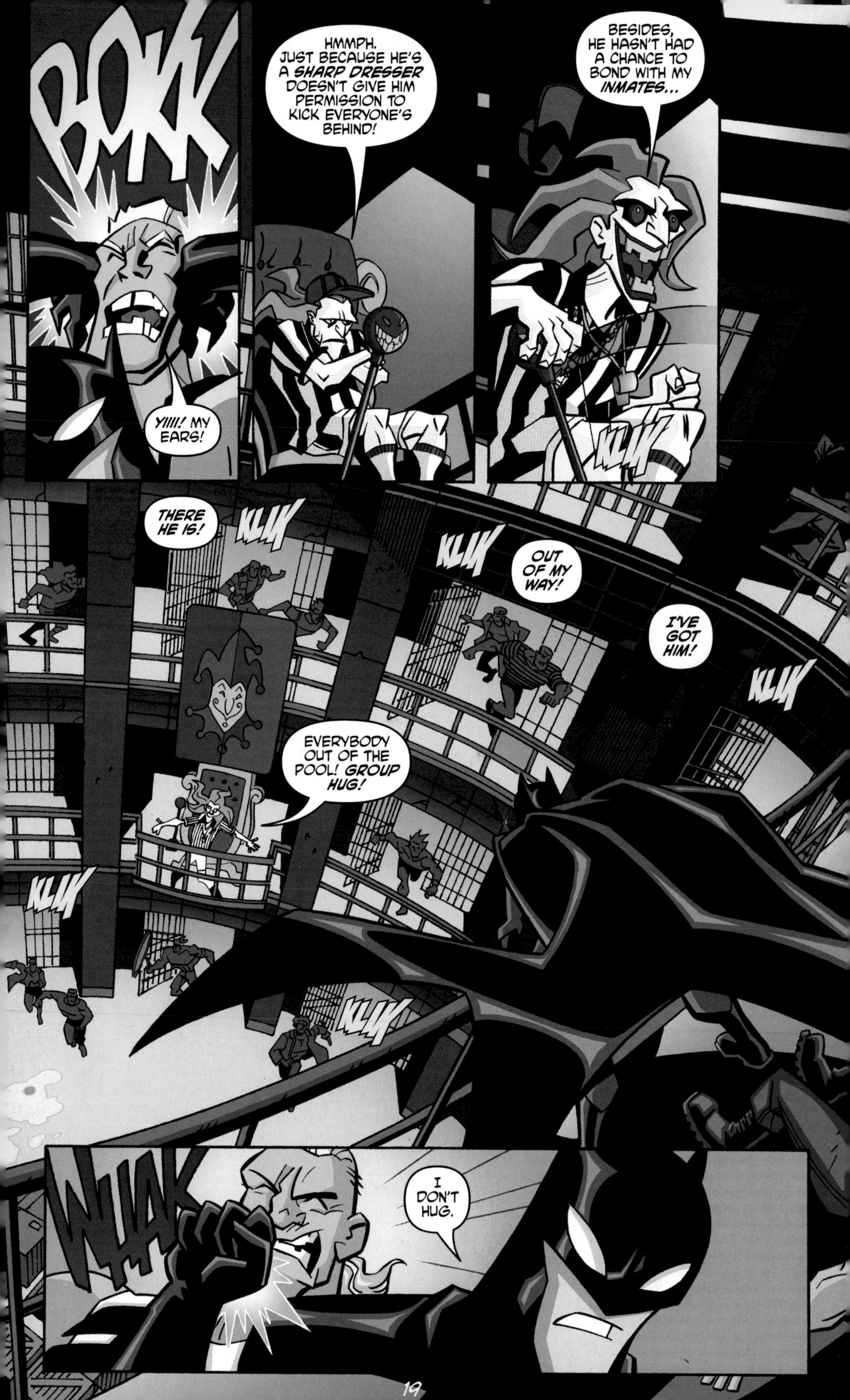
BOOK
YIIII! MY EARS!
HMMPH. JUST BECAUSE HE'S A SHARP DRESSER DOESN'T GIVE HIM PERMISSION TO KICK EVERYONE'S BEHIND!
BESIDES, HE HASN'T HAD A CHANCE TO BOND WITH MY INMATES...
KLIK
THERE HE IS!
KLIK
KLIK
OUT OF MY WAY!
I'VE GOT HIM!
KLIK
EVERYBODY OUT OF THE POOL! GROUP HUG!
KLIK
KLIK
WHAK
I DON'T HUG.

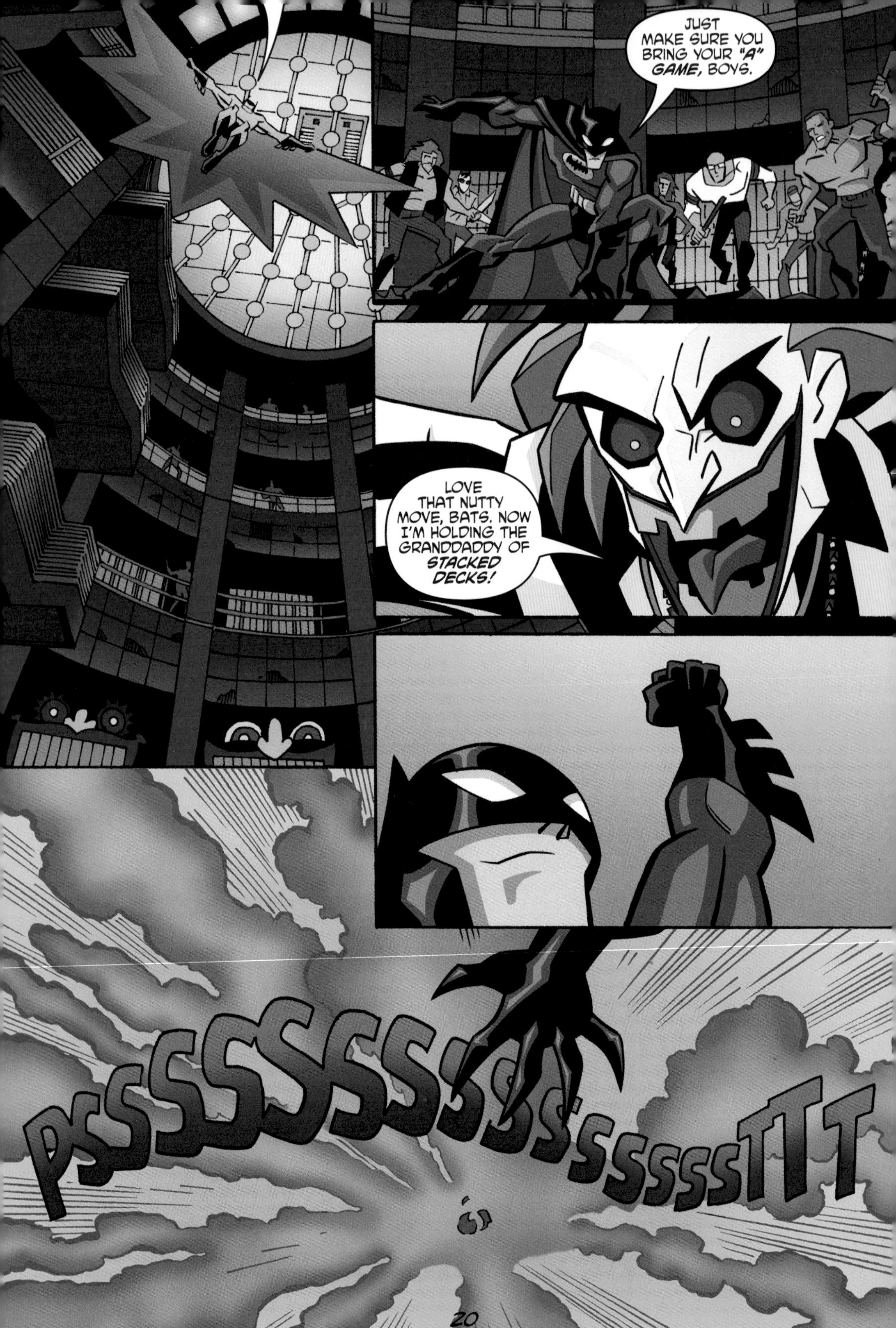
JUST MAKE SURE YOU BRING YOUR "A" GAME, BOYS.
LOVE THAT NUTTY MOVE, BATS. NOW I'M HOLDING THE GRANDDADDY OF STACKED DECKS!
PSSSSSSSSSSSSSSSSSTTT

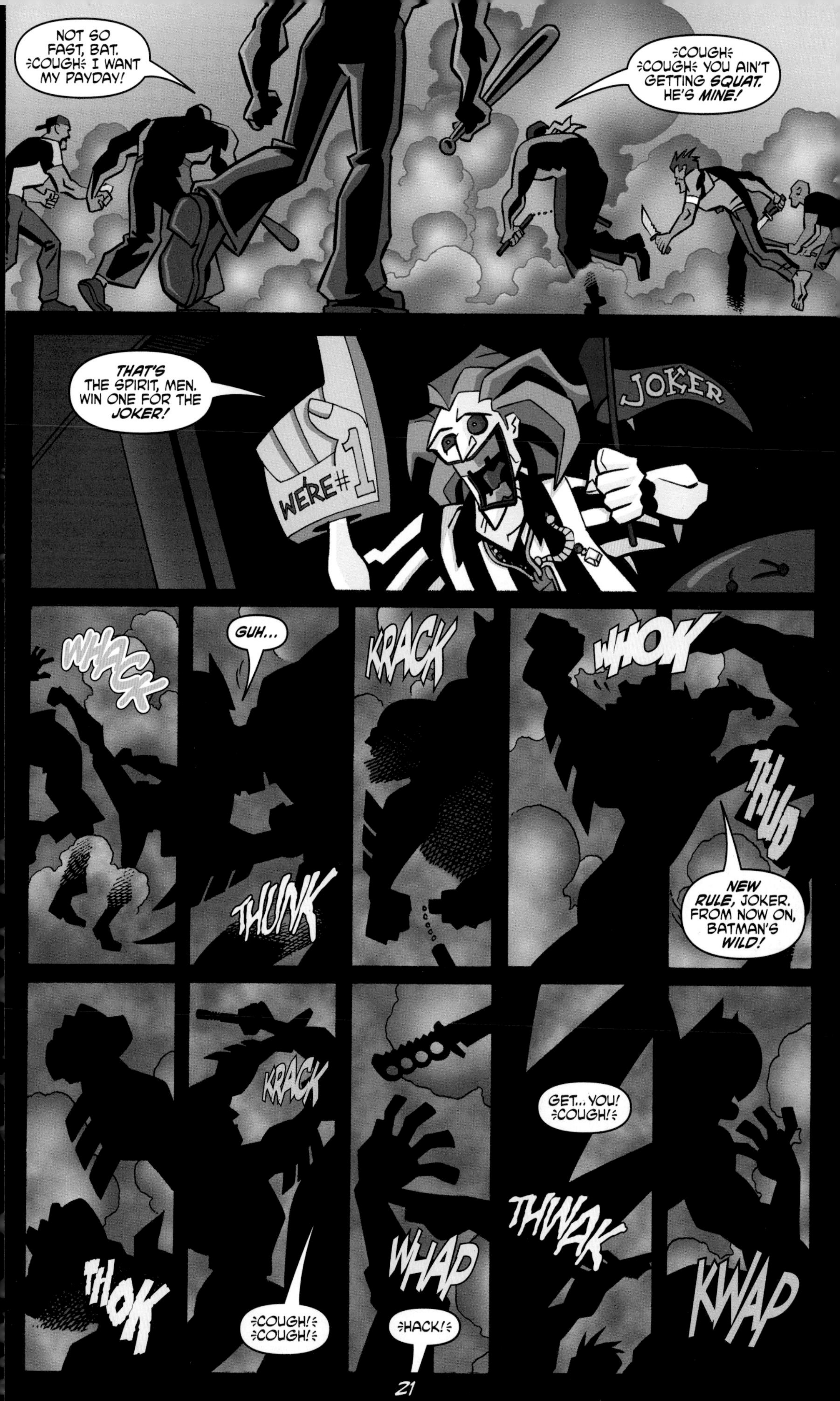
NOT SO FAST, BAT. ⸗COUGH⸗ I WANT MY PAYDAY!
⸗COUGH⸗ ⸗COUGH⸗ YOU AIN'T GETTING SQUAT. HE'S MINE!
THAT'S THE SPIRIT, MEN. WIN ONE FOR THE JOKER!
JOKER
WE'RE #1
WHACK
GUH...
THUNK
KRACK
WHOK
THUD
NEW RULE, JOKER. FROM NOW ON, BATMAN'S WILD!
KRACK
GET... YOU! ⸗COUGH!⸗
THOK
⸗COUGH!⸗ ⸗COUGH!⸗
WHAP
⸗HACK!⸗
THWAK
KWAP

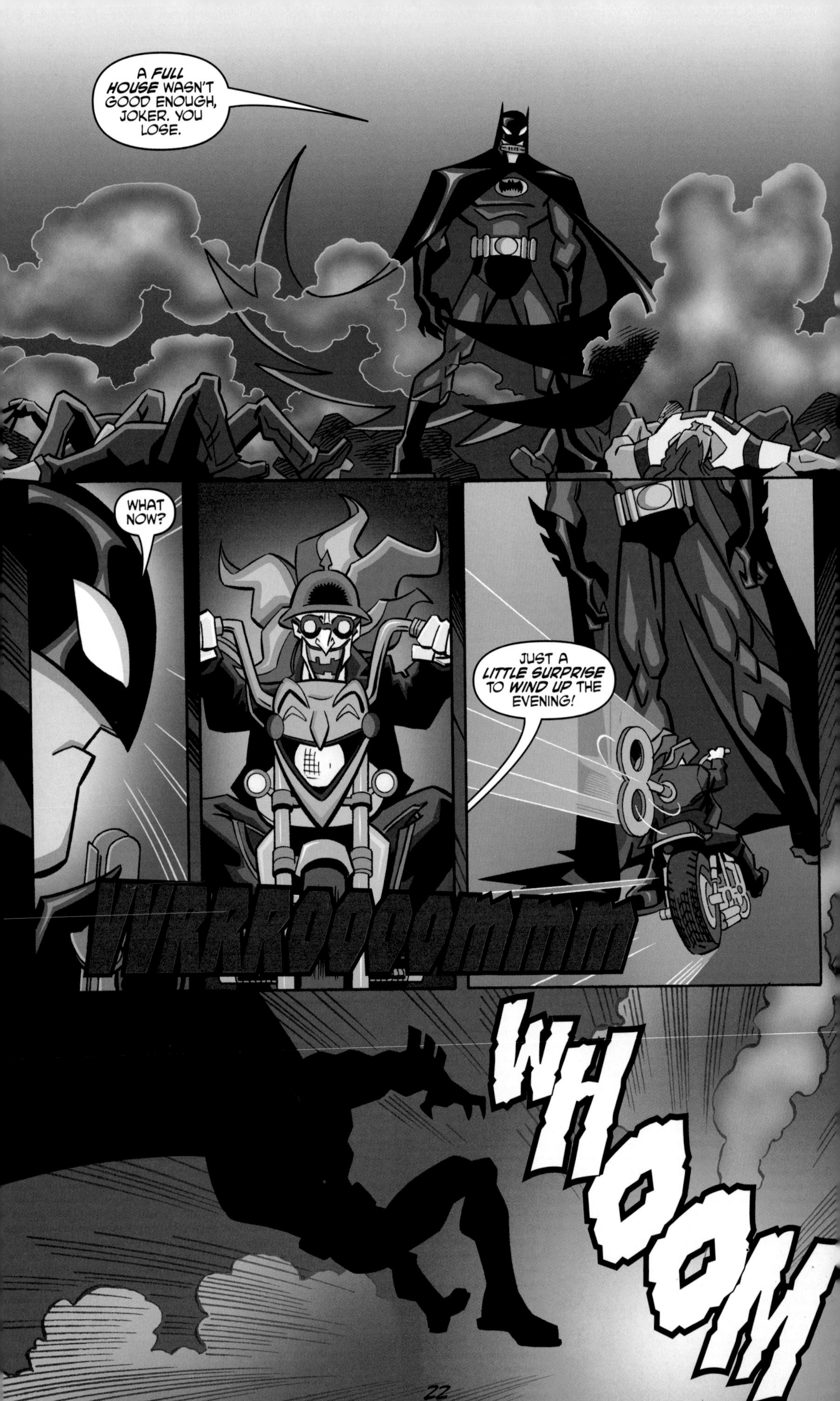
A FULL HOUSE WASN'T GOOD ENOUGH, JOKER. YOU LOSE.
WHAT NOW?
JUST A LITTLE SURPRISE TO WIND UP THE EVENING!
VVRRROOOOOMMMM
WHOOOM

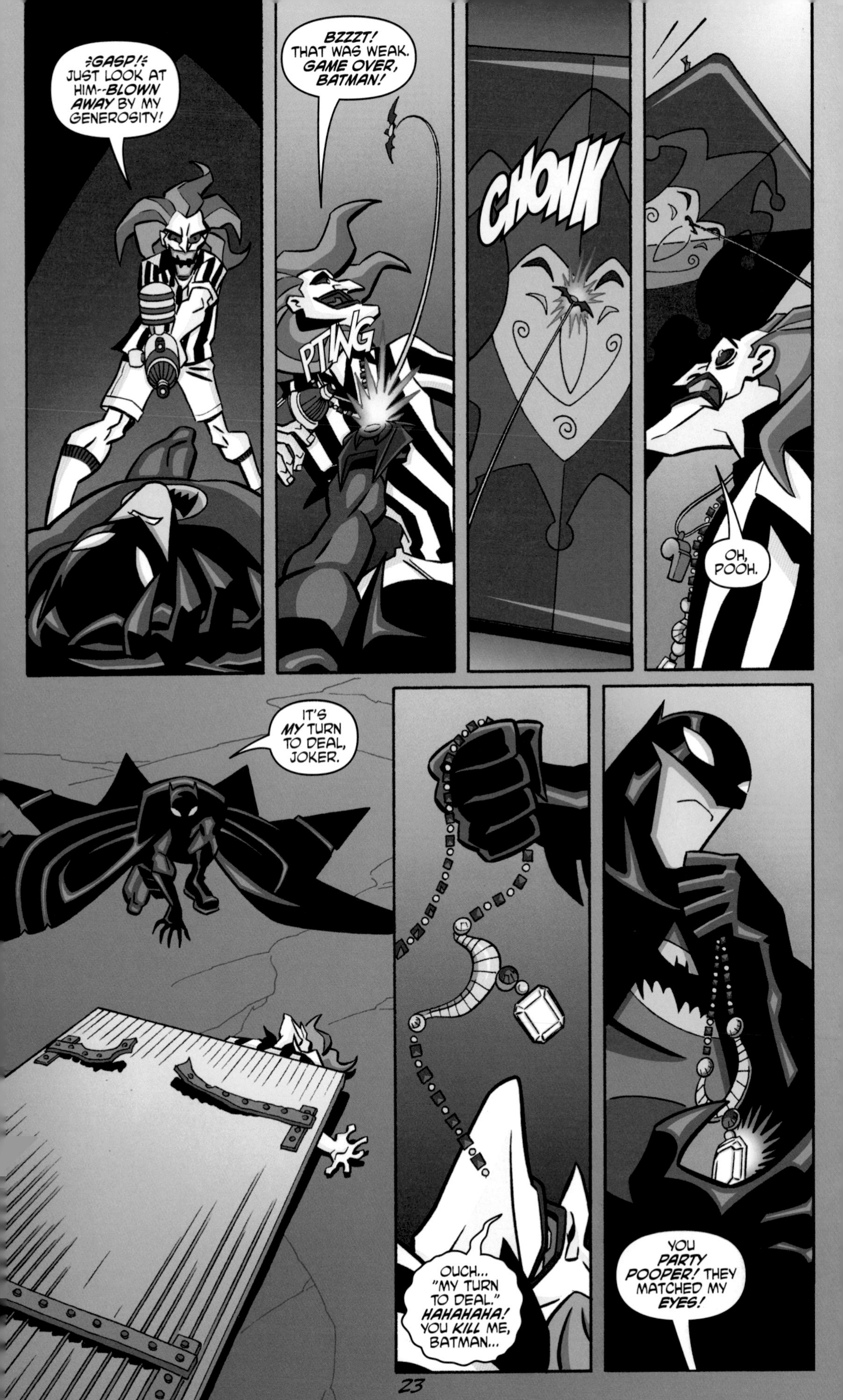

GASP! JUST LOOK AT HIM--BLOWN AWAY BY MY GENEROSITY!
BZZZT! THAT WAS WEAK. GAME OVER, BATMAN!
PTING
CHONK
OH, POOH.
IT'S MY TURN TO DEAL, JOKER.
OUCH... "MY TURN TO DEAL." HAHAHAHA! YOU KILL ME, BATMAN...
YOU PARTY POOPER! THEY MATCHED MY EYES!

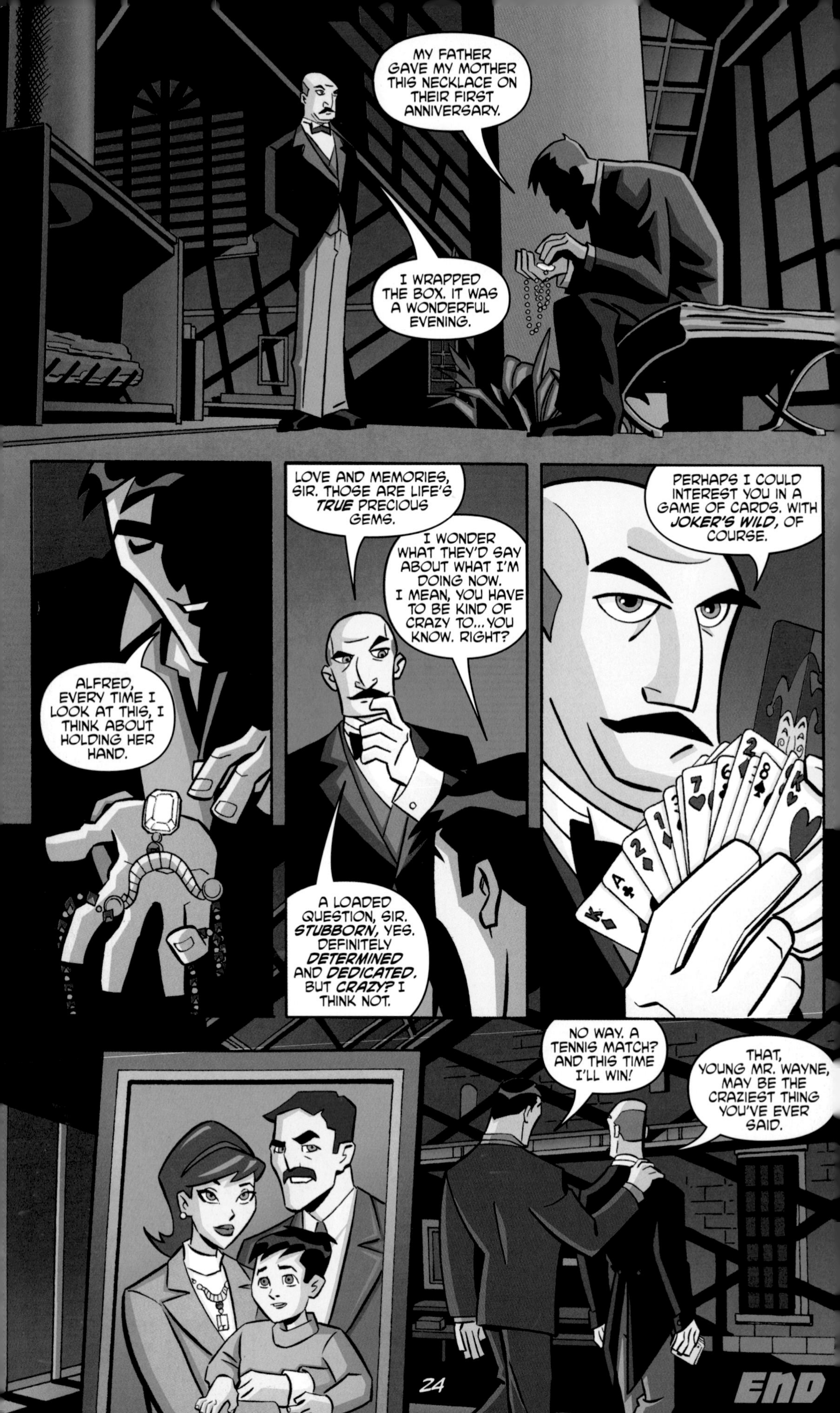
MY FATHER GAVE MY MOTHER THIS NECKLACE ON THEIR FIRST ANNIVERSARY.
I WRAPPED THE BOX. IT WAS A WONDERFUL EVENING.
ALFRED, EVERY TIME I LOOK AT THIS, I THINK ABOUT HOLDING HER HAND.
LOVE AND MEMORIES, SIR. THOSE ARE LIFE'S *TRUE* PRECIOUS GEMS.
I WONDER WHAT THEY'D SAY ABOUT WHAT I'M DOING NOW. I MEAN, YOU HAVE TO BE KIND OF CRAZY TO... YOU KNOW. RIGHT?
A LOADED QUESTION, SIR. *STUBBORN,* YES. DEFINITELY *DETERMINED* AND *DEDICATED.* BUT *CRAZY?* I THINK NOT.
PERHAPS I COULD INTEREST YOU IN A GAME OF CARDS. WITH *JOKER'S WILD,* OF COURSE.
NO WAY. A TENNIS MATCH? AND THIS TIME I'LL WIN!
THAT, YOUNG MR. WAYNE, MAY BE THE CRAZIEST THING YOU'VE EVER SAID.
END

CREATORS

BILL MATHENY WRITER

Along with comics like THE BATMAN STRIKES, Bill Matheny has written for TV series including KRYPTO THE SUPERDOG, WHERE'S WALDO, A PUP NAMED SCOOBY-DOO, and many others.

CHRISTOPHER JONES PENCILLER

Christopher Jones is an artist that has worked for DC Comics, Image, Malibu, Caliber, and Sundragon Comics.

TERRY BEATTY INKER

Terry Beatty has inked THE BATMAN STRIKES! and BATMAN: THE BRAVE AND THE BOLD as well as several other DC Comics graphic novels.

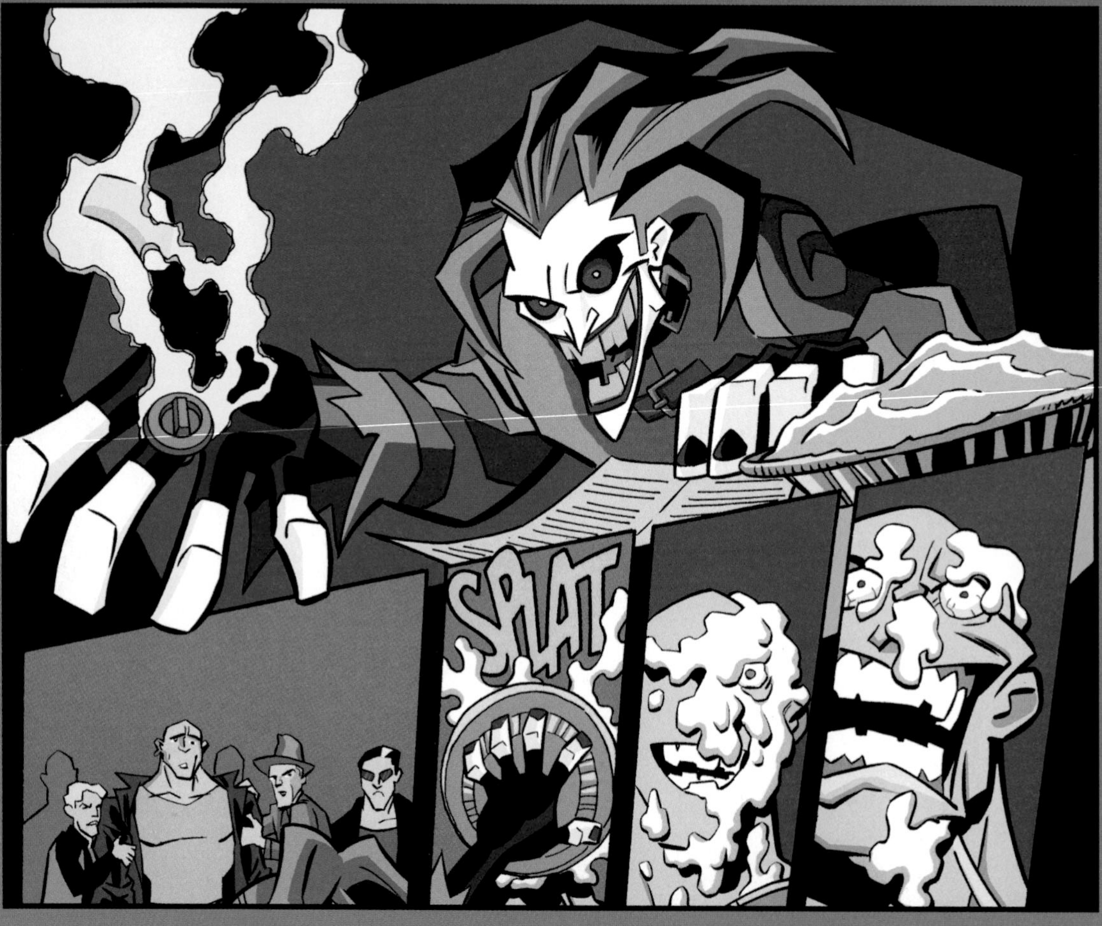
SPLAT

GLOSSARY

bonding (BAHN-ding)--closely connecting with someone

circuits (SUR-kitz)--complete paths that electrical currents can flow around

competitive (kuhm-PET-uh-tiv)--closely contested

concussion (kuhk-KUSH-uhn)--an injury to the brain caused by head trauma

dedicated (ded-uh-KAY-tid)--if you are dedicated, you give a lot of time and energy to something

determined (di-TUR-mind)--if you are determined to do something, you've made a firm decision to do it

generosity (jen-uh-ROSS-i-tee)--the practice of being giving

lame (LAYM)--weak or unconvincing

likewise (LIKE-wize)--also, or in the same way

precious (PRESH-uhss)--rare and valuable, or very special

recruits (ri-KROOTZ)--individuals who have recently joined a group

scramble (SKRAM-buhl)--to mix up

secure (si-KYOOR)--safe, firmly closed, or well protected

VISUAL QUESTIONS & PROMPTS

1. In order to show that the Joker is singing in these panels, the artists included music notes next to the text. What are some other ways they could have shown that Joker was singing?

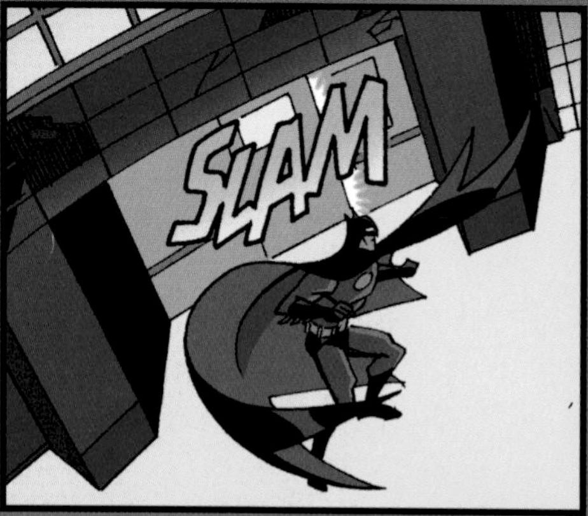
SLAM

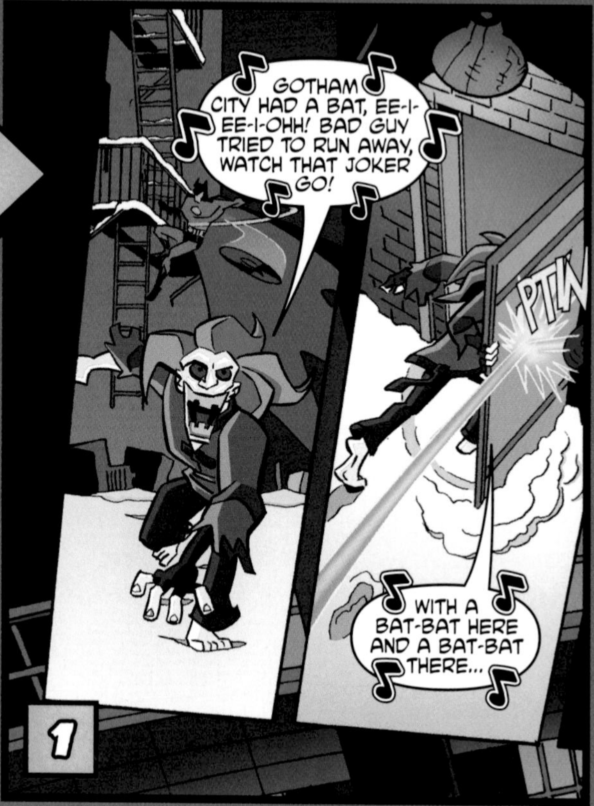
GOTHAM CITY HAD A BAT, EE-I-EE-I-OHH! BAD GUY TRIED TO RUN AWAY, WATCH THAT JOKER GO!
WITH A BAT-BAT HERE AND A BAT-BAT THERE...
1

2. Joker likes making puns, or words that have two meanings. Identify the two words in these two panels that are puns.

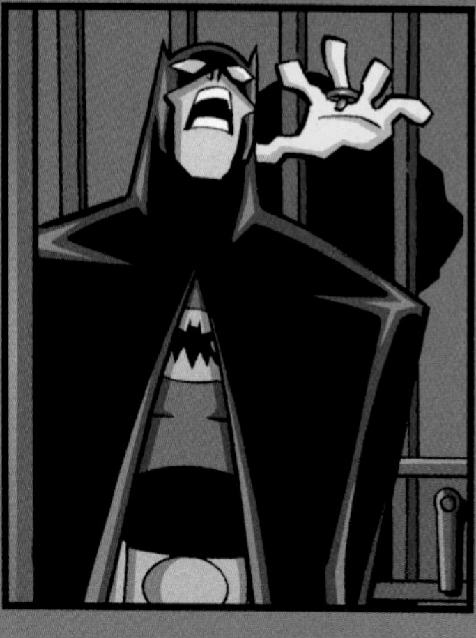

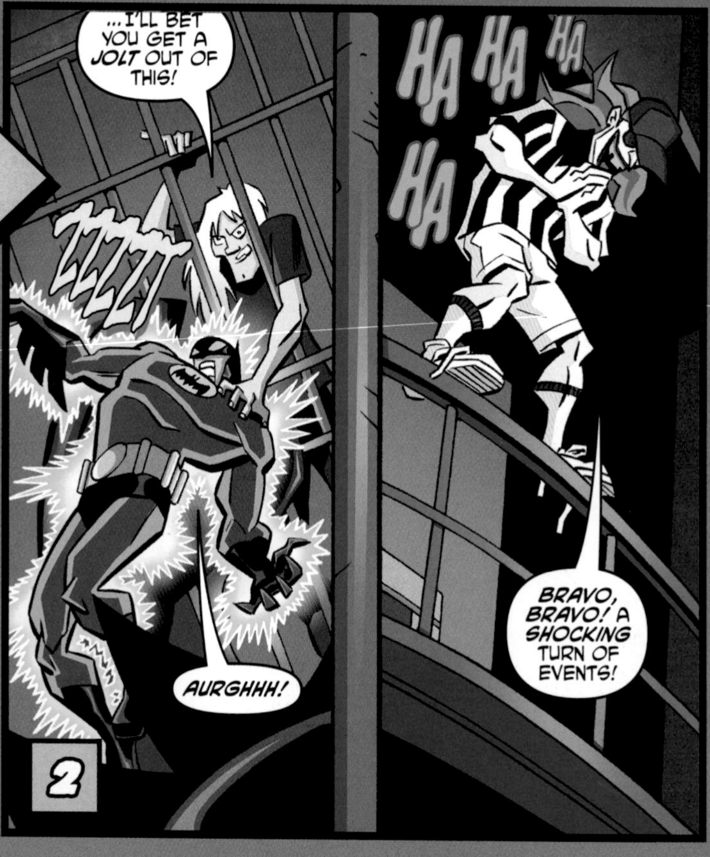
...I'LL BET YOU GET A *JOLT* OUT OF THIS!
ZZZZT
AURGHHH!
HA HA HA HA
BRAVO, BRAVO! A SHOCKING TURN OF EVENTS!
2

3. In this panel, we see the card the Joker has thrown crossing over the borders of the other panels. How does this effect make you feel when you read it? Why do you think the artists chose to illustrate it this way?

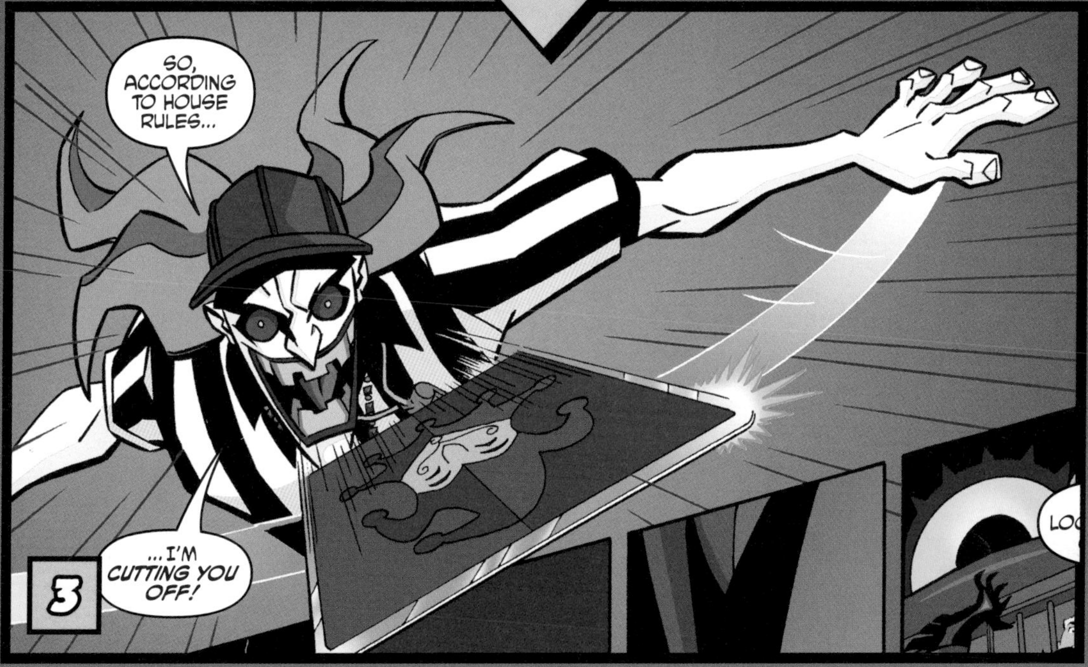

SO, ACCORDING TO HOUSE RULES...
...I'M CUTTING YOU OFF!
3

4. In this spread, the artists used different panel borders than on the other spreads. What are these panel borders, and why do you think the artists chose to depict them in this way?

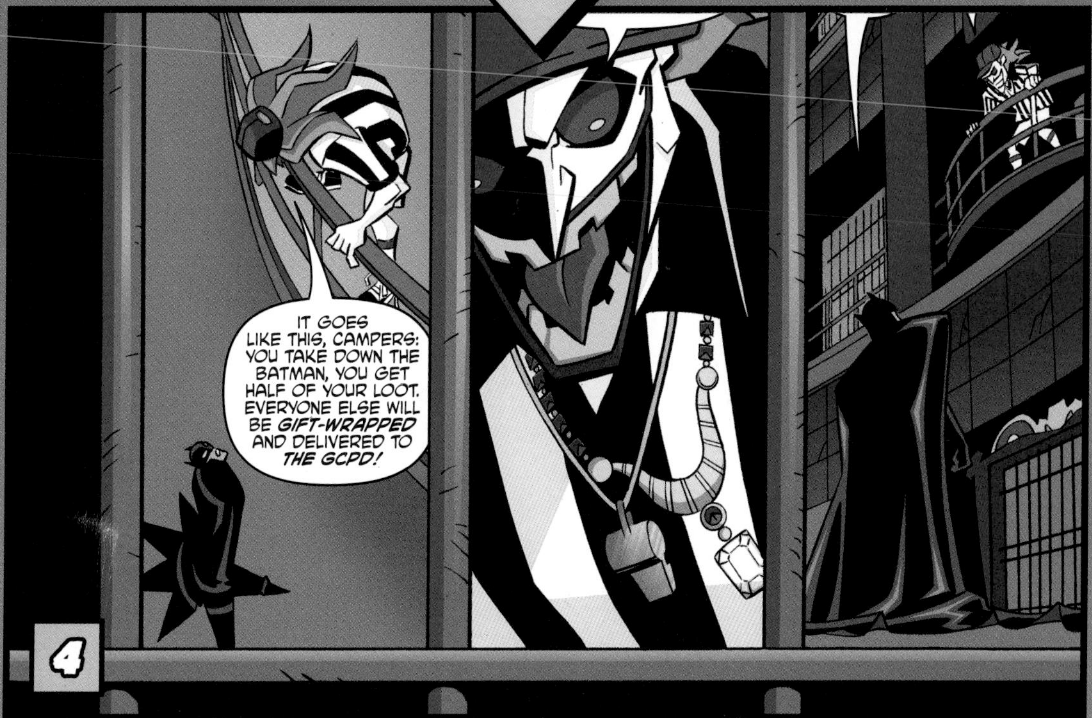

IT GOES LIKE THIS, CAMPERS: YOU TAKE DOWN THE BATMAN, YOU GET HALF OF YOUR LOOT. EVERYONE ELSE WILL BE GIFT-WRAPPED AND DELIVERED TO THE GCPD!
4

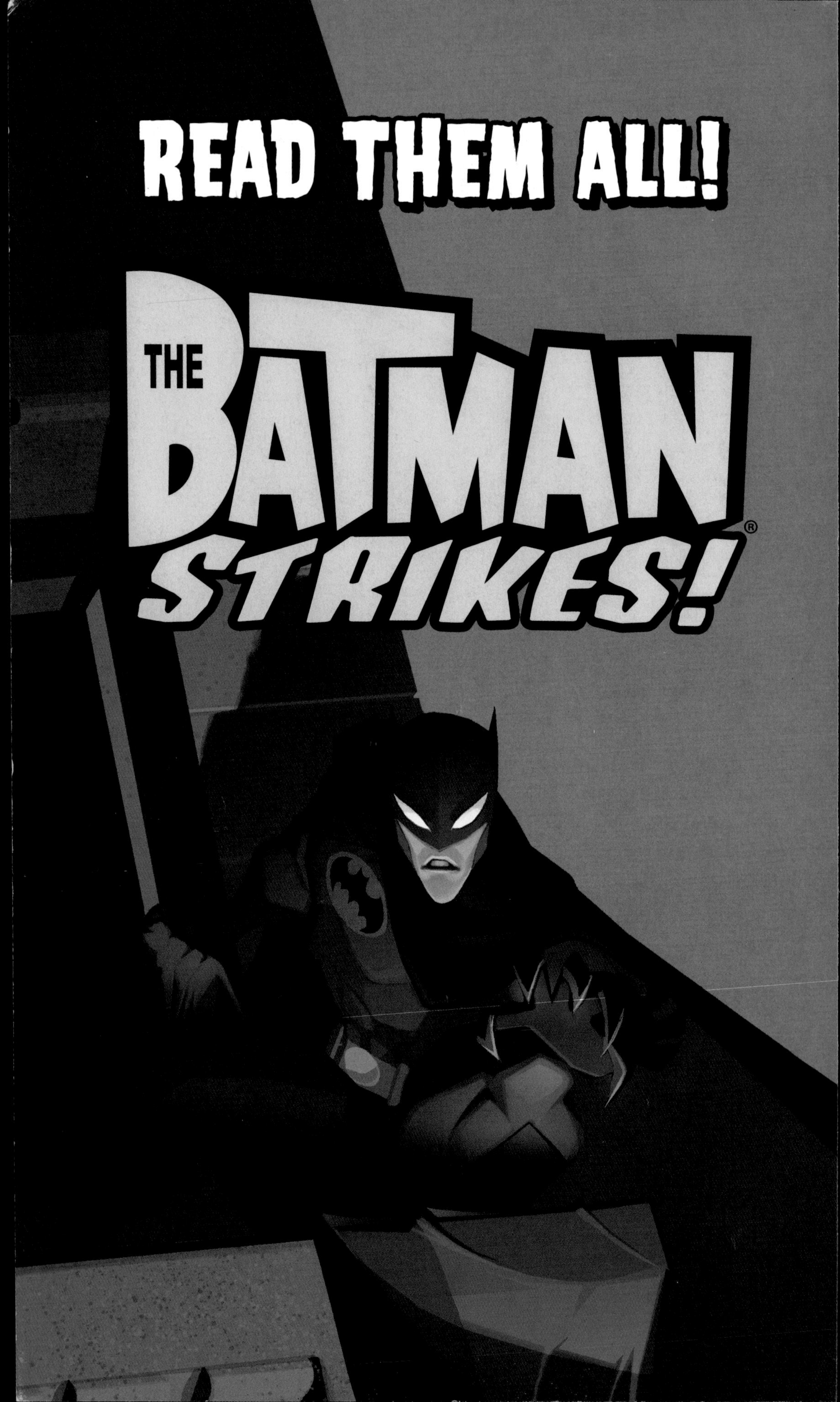
READ THEM ALL!
THE BATMAN STRIKES!

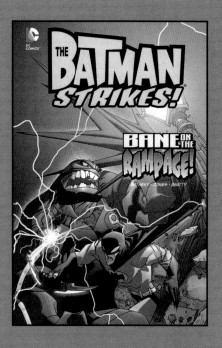

THE BATMAN STRIKES!®

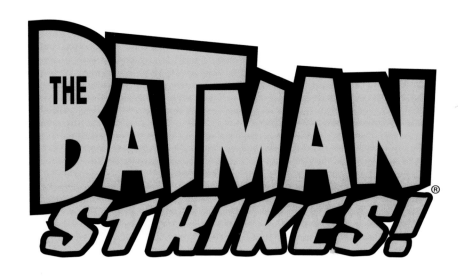